To

MeKenzie с love

Gleeson

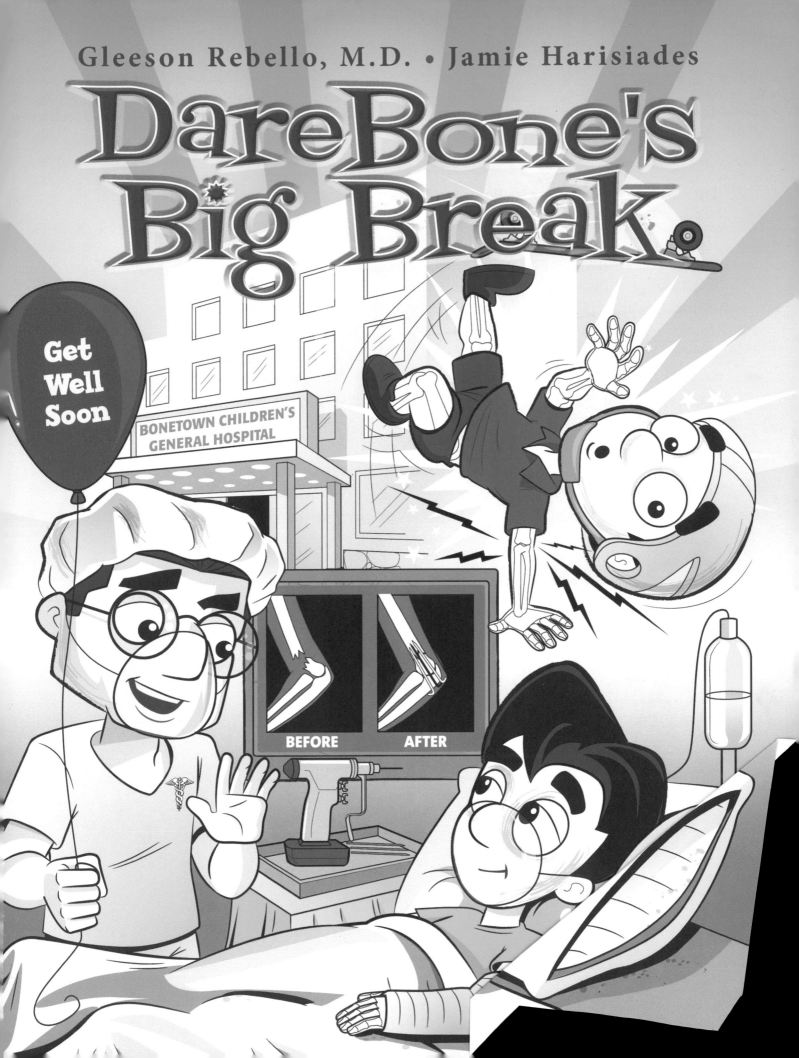

 SDP Publishing

DareBone's Big Break, Published June, 2013

Interior and Cover Illustrations: Randy Jennings
Interior Layout: Howard Communigrafix, Inc.
Editorial and Proofreading: Eden Rivers Editorial Services
Photo Credits: T. Spoon Photography

Published by SDP Publishing, an imprint of SDP Publishing Solutions, LLC.

For more information about this book contact Lisa Akoury-Ross by email at lross@SDPPublishing.com.

To obtain permission(s) to use material from this work, please submit a written request to:

SDP Publishing
Permissions Department
36 Captain's Way, East Bridgewater, MA 02333
or email your request to info@SDPPublishing.com.

ISBN-13: 978-0-9889381-4-4 (hardcover)

Printed in the United States of America

Acknowledgments

Gleeson Rebello would like to acknowledge:

My coauthor, Jamie, who gave a bunch of abstract thoughts a skeleton on which we built a body. My deepest gratitude to the Pediatric Orthopedic Team in the MassGeneral Hospital for Children, for making serious work fun, and for providing constant encouragement in this venture. I also would like to acknowledge the Department of Orthopedic Surgery, Massachusetts General Hospital, and the MassGeneral Hospital for Children for being great places to work, and encouraging outside of the box thinking.

A big thank you to all the great healthcare professionals that I have worked with on multiple continents, who take care of complex problems with a combination of competence, sensitivity, and humor.

Jamie Harisiades would like to acknowledge:

My coauthor, Gleeson, for initiating this journey and being a most supportive guide. My coworkers, mentors, and role models at Massachusetts General Hospital, both past and present, who continue to fuel my passions and shape my path. Andrew, for being my sounding board and constant support.

We would both like to thank the publishing team: Lisa Ann Schleipfer for providing structure to our thoughts, Randy Jennings for creating pictures out of our words, Howard Johnson for turning our project into a dynamic book, and Lisa Akoury-Ross for turning our dream into a solid reality.

Disclaimer

This book is dedicated to all the children that bring meaning to my work; to Rahul and Natasha and their mom, Anu, who give meaning to my life; to my parents Francis and Sicletica, who gave me the gift of life; and to my sister, Gleena, my childhood partner in rhyme.

To Mum and Dad, for teaching me how to pull myself up by the bootstraps after my falls, and to my big brother, Ryan, for showing me where to find the joy and humor in life's inevitable breaks and scrapes.

Hello, my name is DareBone,
I'm daring, yes it's true.
I break my bones so often,
I wish I could fix them with glue.

Children do not choose their parents, they say.
And pets can't choose their owners—not okay!

My best friend, Wag-A-Bone, is a grumpy old mutt,
who cannot keep his drooling mouth shut.
Whenever a thought lights up his head,
his tail says nothing, his tongue wags instead.

Together we run, jump, and play most of the time,
and spend the rest of it making up silly rhyme.
Our friendship is great; we have a special spark,
even though my furry friend has quite a snarky bark!

I ask my Mom, "I'd really like, if I may,
to ride my bicycle to the playground today!"
"Yes, of course," Mom says, "what a wonderful plan.
But you must be careful and wear your helmet, little man!"

My friends were waiting for us to play.
"Hello, DareBone, we're having fun today!"
We jump right in and start the game,
"This is so much fun!" I exclaim.

10

At the playground I frolic, taking tumbles galore.
With fumbles and stumbles, the dirt I explore.

My hands slip and I fall from the jungle gym!
Oh no! This plunge is looking quite grim!

I hit the sand with a big bump,
I hope to escape with not more than a lump.
But oh my, I fear my elbow is hurt!
And I've dirtied my pants and torn my shirt!

I don't like to whine; no I don't like to cry.
Because I think I am one real tough guy.
But ...

There he goes: boohoo-hoo!
But I guess a man's got to do what a man's got to do.

Mom appears with her eyes grown wide,
kneeling by me, right by my side.
"Ow! Mom!" I say, "My elbow hurts a whole lot,
right here," I point, "right in this very spot!"

We are in luck, Dr. WonderBone is here!
He hears my cries and rushes near.

Our children's bone doctor is hanging out with his tot.
A business move to round up patients I hope it is not.

"DareBone, I'm going to examine your arm.
I promise to be gentle and do you no harm.
Now give me a thumbs up, an A-OK, now make a peace sign.
Use your fingers like scissors and cut along a line."

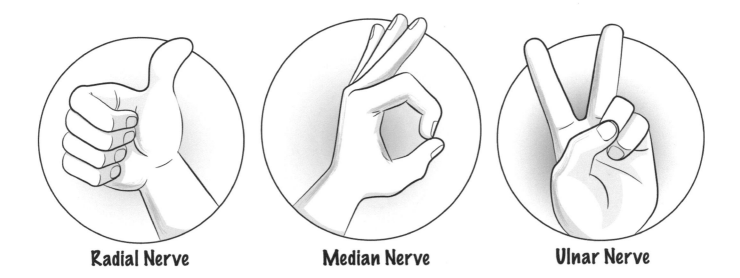

Radial Nerve   Median Nerve   Ulnar Nerve

"Can you feel me touch your fingertips?" I reply with a "yes."

"Good!" he says, "Your nerves are in one piece,
but your bone might be a mess."

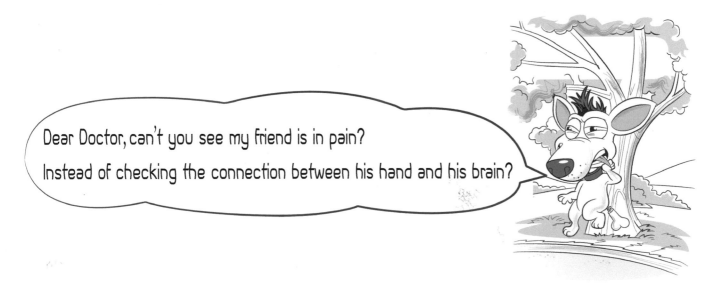

Dear Doctor, can't you see my friend is in pain?
Instead of checking the connection between his hand and his brain?

"We'll splint his arm to keep the bones from shifting.
For surgery, into sleep he will be drifting.
Starting now, he can have nothing to eat or drink.
Surgery it is for this little guy; yes, that's what I think."

Dr. WonderBone carefully splints my arm,
to keep it safe from any future harm.

To the BoneTown Children's General Hospital we go.
Dr. WonderBone works there; it is the best, we know!

BZZZZZZZZZ BZZZZZZZZZ

18

So many kids in the Emergency Room today:
Jack broke his forearm during a three-legged relay,
Jenny fell off a bunk bed and broke her wrist,
and Jill hurt her ankle while dancing the twist!

PICK-A-BONE HEALTH CARE

After X-rays, the kids will get their casts,
but these things don't happen very fast.
The doctors and nurses are very busy,
and the ER sometimes gets into a tizzy.
Patiently they all sit and wait,
knowing the staff has a lot on their plate.

My name is called and it's time for an X-ray.
Nurse TenderBone is nice and shows us the way.
"A picture of your bones is what the machine will take,
so we can see where your bone has a break."

Why does he need an X-ray? His bones can be seen!
He doesn't even need a costume to go out on Halloween!

The X-ray machine whirrs, beeps, and clicks.
I must keep my arm still, so there won't be any tricks.
The X-ray is quick, and doesn't hurt me at all!
I'm proud of myself; I stand nice and tall!

There's a knock at the door; Dr. WonderBone smiles.
"Hello there, DareBone, I've had a look at your files!"
A click on the computer, and my X-ray fills the screen.
"Looks like your elbow is broken, Mr. Jumpin' Bean!"

"For a while you won't be able to play
quite as hard as you did today.
I know that this comes with a bit of frustration,
and it seems scary, but you need an operation."

"We'll fix your elbow with pins, and put your arm in a cast,
and then the four weeks' time will fly by nice and fast!
When you return we'll take the pins out from your elbow,
and before you know it, you'll be good as new, little fellow!"

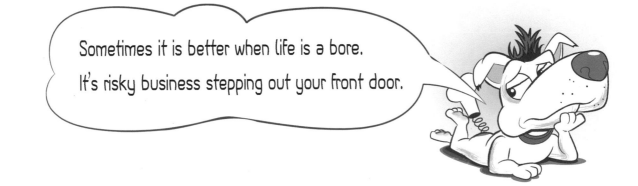

Sometimes it is better when life is a bore.
It's risky business stepping out your front door.

25

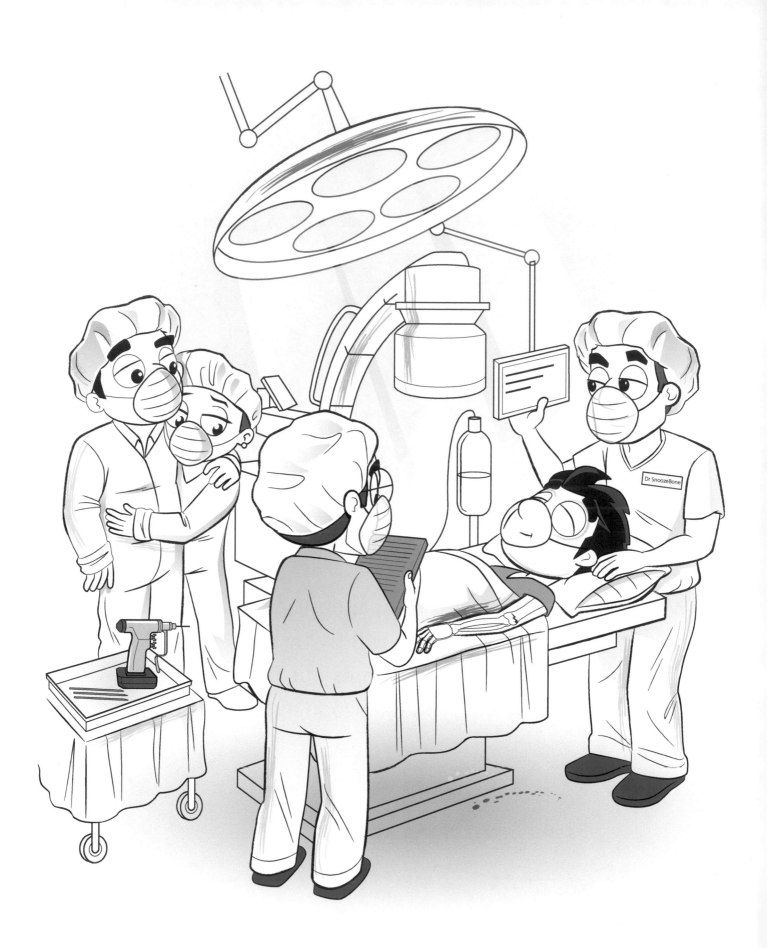

A few hours later I am in the operating suite.
I am really hungry 'cause I've had nothing to eat.
Mom gives me a smile; the lights are quite bright.
She pats my good arm, and tells me I'll be all right.

Dr. SnoozeBone tells me jokes that make me giggle,
and puts a bubblegum-smelling mask over my face while I wriggle.
He says, "Think of a nice place you might want to go!"
My body feels heavy, but I go with the flow.

I remember not much, into sleep I do slide.
I wake up with Mom and Dad by my side.
Dad pats my arm, Mom kisses my cheek.
I feel pretty good, though maybe just a bit weak.

Dr. WonderBone visits to say I'll be staying the night.
"The night nurse is nice! Don't worry, she won't bite!"
Mom and Dad will stay on cots near my bed.
I can't wait until morning when I can be fed.

Home again, home again, the next day I go.

The nurses tell me that I'll need to move slow.

Dr. WonderBone says, "See you in four weeks just about!"

We make an appointment and then we head out.

The cast is annoying and my lesson I do learn:
When falling off the jungle gym, a cast you will earn.
We return to the clinic after a few weeks' time.
My cast smells so bad, I bet it's growing slime.

Never known a moment when he ever smelled yummy.
His cast now stinks like the gas in my tummy.

They went in a blur these four weeks in the cast.
Back to Dr. WonderBone's office we are at last.
We give my name at the desk and wait for a while,
but I'm getting my cast off, so I wait with a big smile!

Patience is a virtue there is absolutely no doubt.
Doctors' offices are where these lessons are handed out!

31

Dr. WonderBone says, "Hey! Your X-rays look good!
MerryBone will cut off your cast like I would saw wood."
The saw buzzes a bit, and tickles my whole arm.
It sounds real scary, but it does me no harm.

The cast comes off like one, two, three,
and Dr. WonderBone tries to crack a joke for me.
"I'll pull the pins out, and it won't hurt ME one bit!"
I like it when he is funny, I must admit.
There are a few drops of blood, really, that's all.
It is uncomfortable, not painful, and I don't even bawl.

My elbow is a little stiff, and I'm nervous to move it at all.
I stay away from the rough play, so I don't stumble or fall.
Wag-A-Bone and I take a few weeks off 'til we're back to our old ways,
and then we're running, jumping, and playing most of our days!

35

About the Authors

Gleeson Rebello, M.D., is on staff in the Department of Orthopedic Surgery at Massachusetts General Hospital, is a Pediatric Orthopedic Surgeon at the MassGeneral Hospital for Children, and also has been a member of the faculty at Harvard Medical School since 2008. He has trained extensively in India and in the U.S., and has vast experience in treating various childhood injuries and other pediatric orthopedic conditions.

Jamie Harisiades is a New Hampshire native, Boston transplant, Middlebury College graduate, and aspiring physician. She currently works in Breast Oncology Clinical Research at Massachusetts General Hospital and plans to attend medical school in the near future. She is the daughter of Judi and Greg Harisiades and sister to Ryan Harisiades.

Hey kids! Did you love *DareBone's Big Break*? Do you want to learn more about DareBone and his friends?

Be sure to visit our website at

www.darebonesbigbreak.com

And don't forget to check out our Facebook page

www.facebook.com/Darebone

Have questions or comments about DareBone's elbow break?
Ask Dr. WonderBone! Send email to **drwonderbone@darebones.com**.

Copies of *DareBone's Big Break* available now!

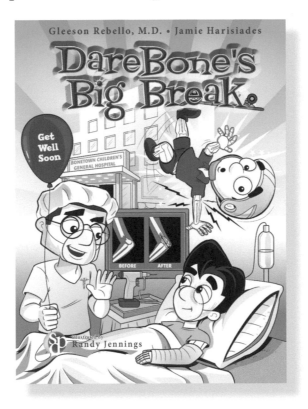

For general order inquires and ordering instructions visit

http://sdppublishingsolutions.com/bookstore/

Also available on: Amazon.com, BarnesAndNoble.com

Hospitals and special interest groups interested in ordering, please contact
SDP Publishing Solutions directly.
Email us at: **info@SDPPublishing.com**, or call **617-775-0656**.

CPSIA information can be obtained
at www.ICGtesting.com
Printed in the USA
BVHW020917051219
565180BV00006B/5/P